Moo BaaBaa Quack

Written by Francesca Simon

Illustrated by Emily Bolam

Orion
Children's Books

CONTENTS

Food + Farming

Big Woods

Thistle Meadow

old Barn

POTTER'S BARN

Orchard

For my favourite musicians
David Abell and Seann Alderking
and my favourite diva, Patti LuPone.

With thanks to Jane Gillie for
the *Big Fat Pig* song.

F.S.

Book design by Tracey Cunnell

First published in Great Britain in 1997
by Orion Children's Books
a division of the Orion Publishing Group Ltd
Orion House
5 Upper St Martin's Lane
London WC2H 9EA

Text copyright © Francesca Simon 1997
Illustrations copyright © Emily Bolam 1997

The right of Francesca Simon and Emily Bolam
to be identified as the author and illustrator
respectively of this work has been asserted.

A catalogue record for this book
is available from the British Library
Printed in Italy

Big Woods

Thistle Meadow

old Barn

POTTER'S
~ BARN ~

Orchard

For my favourite musicians
David Abell and Seann Alderking
and my favourite diva, Patti LuPone.

With thanks to Jane Gillie for
the *Big Fat Pig* song.

F.S.

Book design by Tracey Cunnell

First published in Great Britain in 1997
by Orion Children's Books
a division of the Orion Publishing Group Ltd
Orion House
5 Upper St Martin's Lane
London WC2H 9EA

A catalogue record for this book
is available from the British Library
Printed in Italy

Runaway
Duckling

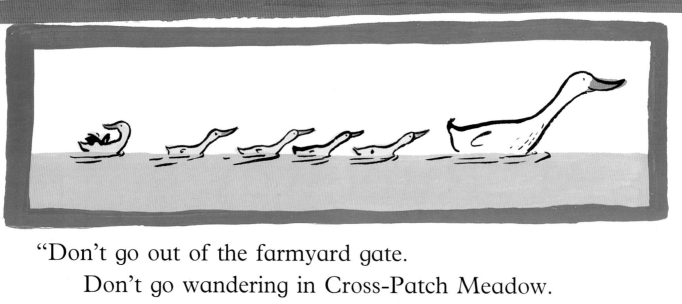

"Don't go out of the farmyard gate.
Don't go wandering in Cross-Patch Meadow.
Don't go to Far Away Field.
Don't go near Snapdragon Pond.
And don't go in the old barn with the
peeling pink front door," said Mother Duck.
"It's dangerous."

"Yes Mum," said the first duckling.

"Yes Mum," said the second duckling.

"Yes Mum," said the third duckling.

"Yes Mum," said the fourth duckling.

But the fifth duckling said nothing.

"Don't, don't, don't, don't, don't," she grumbled. "Why shouldn't I go and see all those places? I'm old enough, and I'm big enough."

While the other ducklings went paddling with their mother in Muddy Pond, the fifth duckling zipped across Butterfly Field and Silver Meadow towards the farmyard gate.

Then she hopped through the railings and waddled into the lane.

"Wow!" said the duckling. "It's great out here."

A milk lorry and a haycart swerved to avoid the duckling as she stood in the middle of the road.

BEEP! BEEP! BEEP!

"Cheep, cheep, cheep!" chirped the duckling, waving to them.

13

Then she strolled along into Cross-Patch Meadow.
She was too young to read the sign saying:

DANGER! RAGING BULL!

"Isn't this a pretty meadow!" said the duckling. "And what a great place for a picnic. Silly Mum telling me not to come here," she added, popping through the hedgerow into Far Away Field.

She stopped to shake a
pebble off her webbed foot,
and didn't notice Samson
the Tractor chugging along
towards her.

VROOM VROOM VROOM – PHUT!

"Hello, Samson," said the duckling, looking up. "What are
you doing in the ditch?"

"Grrrr," said Samson.

"Nothing to worry about in Far Away Field," said the duckling. "What an old fusspot Mum is."

The duckling bounced happily along to Snapdragon Pond. Hidden in the dark water, a giant snapping fish waited.

"Great place to swim," said the duckling. "So much nicer than Muddy Pond. I'll jump in right now."

SPLISH-SPLASH SPLISH-SPLASH-PLOP!

"Lovely," said the duckling, shaking herself dry. "I'll tell everyone I've found a great swimming pool."

Then the runaway duckling scampered across Windy Haugh to the old barn, which stood alone and dilapidated in Thistle Meadow.

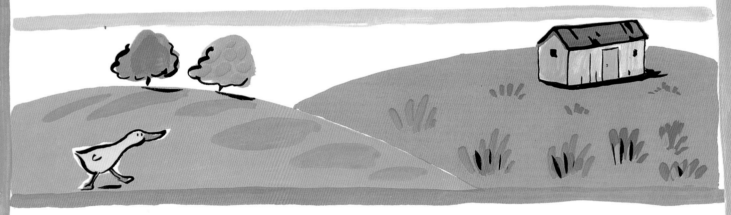

"What a funny looking barn," said the duckling. "I must peep inside."

CREAK CREAK CRE-EEEAK squeaked the old barn door.

"Goodness, it's dark in here," said the duckling.
High above her head, a barn owl stirred.
"Yoo hoo, duckling," called a voice outside.
Who's that? thought the duckling.
"Hello, duckling," said Buster the dog.
"You're far from home."
"Hello, Buster," said the duckling.
"I'm having an adventure."

"It's getting late now. Come on, I'll give you a ride back to Potter's Barn," said Buster.

"Great!" said the duckling.

She felt like a queen as she returned to the farmyard on Buster's back.

"Where have you been?" said Mother Duck. "I've been so worried."

"Everywhere," said the duckling. "Cross-Patch Meadow, Far Away Field, Snapdragon Pond and the old barn."

"WHAT?" said Mother Duck.

"And you know what, Mum? No danger anywhere!"

Baa Baa! Where Are My Lambs?

The lambs were playing tag in Butterfly Field.

"Got you!" bleated Tilly.
"No! I got you," bleated Tam.
"Tilly, Tam," called Mother Sheep.
"Time to come in."
Tilly looked at Tam.
Tam looked at Tilly.

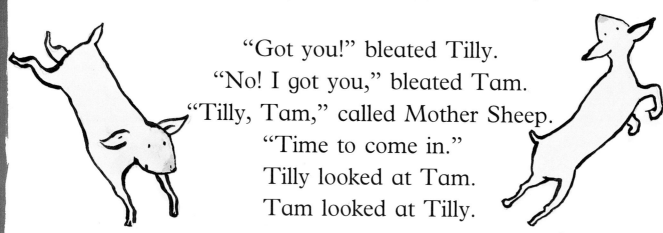

"HIDE!" they baaed, and scrambled behind the water trough.

Mother Sheep looked to the left. No lambs. She looked to the right. No lambs. She looked behind her. Still no lambs.
"Where can those naughty lambs be?" she said.
And off she went to ask Squeaky the cat.

"**BAA BAA!** Where are my lambs?"
Squeaky leapt into the air
and did a somersault.
"*MIAOW MIAOW!* With the cow,"
said Squeaky.

So off went Mother Sheep to Silver Meadow to ask Daffodil.

"BAA BAA! Where are my lambs?"
Daffodil the cow shrugged her shoulders and chewed.
"*MOO MOO!* I haven't a clue," she said.
"Very strange," said Mother Sheep.
"Wait a minute, what's this I see?
It must be my naughty lambs."
She crept up to the hedgerow
and . . . "Got you!" she cried.
"Oops, I've been tricked. It's
just an old tuft of wool. Now
where can those lambs be?"
"Ask Trot. He's sure to
know," said Rosie the calf.

Off went Mother Sheep to the stable.

"**BAA BAA!** Where are my lambs?"
"*NEIGH NEIGH!* Search the hay,"
said Trot the horse, munching some oats.
Mother Sheep saw something sticking up.
Could it be Tilly and Tam's ears?
She sneaked up and . . .
"Got you!" she cried. "Oops.
A saddle. Tricked again.
Where can those lambs be?"
"Try the hens," said Trot.

Off went Mother Sheep to the hen house.

"**BAA BAA!** Where are my lambs?" asked Mother Sheep.
"*CLUCK CLUCK!* Ask a duck," said the hens.
"Wait a minute," said Mother Sheep.
"What's this I see? It looks like Tilly
and Tam's shiny black hooves."
    She sneaked up and . . .
"Got you!" she cried.
"Oops. Wrong again!
It's just a feed scoop.
    Where, oh where, can
those naughty lambs be?"

"There's nobody here but us chickens," said Red Rooster.
So Mother Sheep trotted to Muddy Pond to ask the ducks.

"Shame I can't find Tam and Tilly," she said loudly. "They were going to have a special treat for supper tonight . . . clover! But never mind – all the more for me."

"**BAA BAA!** Where are my lambs?"

"*QUACK QUACK*. Check your back," said the ducks.

Mother Sheep turned round. Her lambs were found, safe and sound!

Billy The Kid Goes Wild

Billy the Kid had big plans. When he had finished munching the blankets he was going to gobble some tasty paper bags he'd seen blowing about in Silver Meadow. Then he wanted to visit Muddy Pond, watch the fish, and nibble some thorny bushes. Then he was off to Gabby Goose's birthday party.

So you can imagine how Billy felt when his father interrupted.

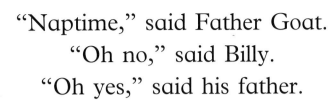

"Naptime," said Father Goat.
"Oh no," said Billy.
"Oh yes," said his father.
"If you don't have a nap you'll be
too tired for Gabby's party."
"No I won't," said Billy.
"Yes you will," said Father Goat.
"But I'm not tired," said Billy.

Trot poked his head over the stable door.
"I'll help Billy feel sleepy," said Trot.
"Come on Billy, I'll race you
across Butterfly Field."

Off they galloped.
"I won," shouted Billy the Kid. "Race you back."
So Trot and Billy zoomed back to the stable.

"Again!" shouted Billy. Back and forth, back and forth they ran. At last Trot stood panting.
"Let's race to Far Away Field," said Billy.

"If you don't mind, Billy, I think I'll just rest for a moment," said Trot, yawning. He closed his eyes and fell asleep.

"Naptime," said Father Goat.
"But I'm not tired,"
said Billy the Kid.
"You're going to be too tired for
Gabby's party," said Father Goat.
"No I'm not," said Billy.

Squeaky the cat scampered over.
"I'll help Billy feel sleepy,"
said Squeaky. "Come on
Billy, let's do somersaults
all the way to Muddy Pond.
Last one there is a ninny."

Off they somersaulted.
"I won," shouted Billy. "Let's race again."
Head over heels they rolled. At last Squeaky stood panting.
"Let's hop backwards to the haystack now," said Billy.

"If you don't mind, Billy," said Squeaky, yawning,
"I think I'll just lie down for a moment."
She closed her eyes and fell asleep.

"Naptime," said Father Goat.
"But I'm still not tired," said Billy.

Buster the dog and Rosie the calf strolled by.

"We'll help Billy feel sleepy," said Buster. "Come on Billy,
let's see who can bellow the loudest."

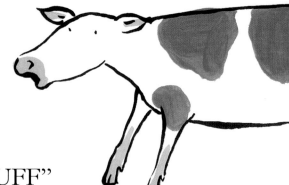

"RUFF RUFF RUFF"

"MOOOOOOOOOOOOOOOOOO"

"MAAAAAAAAAAAAAAAAAAAAAAAAAAA!"

"RUFF RUFF RUFF"

"MOOOOOOOOOOOOOOO"

"MAAAAAAAAAAAAAAAAAAAAAAAA!"

"RUFF RUFF RUFF"

"MOOOOOOOOOOOOOO"

"MAAAAAAAAAAAAAAAAAAAAAA!"

Back and forth across the farmyard they hullabalooed, louder and louder, barking, mooing, and bleating. At last Buster and Rosie stood panting.

"That was fantastic," said Billy the Kid.
"Let's go and play with Tam and Tilly now."
"If you don't mind, Billy, I'll just lie down for a moment," said Buster, yawning.
"Me too," said Rosie. They closed their eyes and fell asleep.

Just then Gabby ran out of her shed, honking.
"Party time!" she yelled.

"Wake up, Trot! Wake up, Squeaky! Wake up, Buster!
Wake up, Rosie!" shouted Billy. "It's party time."

Everyone had a lovely time at Gabby's party. They
played musical statues, pass the parcel, and pin the
hat on the farmer. Then everyone ate lots and lots of
hay and corn and oats.

Well, almost everyone.

Barnyard
Hullabaloo

"COCK A DOODLE DOO!"

"COCK A DOODLE DOO!"

It was morning at Potter's Barn. The animals heard Red Rooster's wake-up call, stretched their legs and rose to start the day.

Someone hiding in Thistle Meadow also heard Red Rooster crowing. That someone was Fox.

"Hmmmmmmm," murmured Fox. "Doesn't that rooster sound plump and juicy?"

He pricked up his ears and listened again.

"COCK A DOODLE *DOO!*"

"CLUCK CLUCK CLUCK!"

"CHEEP CHEEP CHEEP!"

"Ah yes," he added, licking his sharp white teeth. "Fine fat hens and chicks, too. I could fancy a hen, or two, or three, for my dinner, with some tender little chicks for dessert. Indeed I could."

Fox slunk through the long grass of Thistle Meadow and peered down at the farm.

"I think I'll pay Potter's Barn a little visit tonight, heh heh heh." And off he crept.

Buster was dashing round Windy Haugh chasing squirrels when suddenly he sniffed a strange stinky whiff. He raised his head and saw the top of Fox's red tail bobbing in and out of the grass.

Fox is back, thought Buster. I'd better warn the others.

Meanwhile, the Potter's Barn Band were rehearsing a new song, "Barnyard Lullaby".

"Everyone ready?" said Belle the pig.
"Let's take it from the top. Ah-one, Ah-two:"

MAAA MAAA!

BAAAAA!

MOOO MOOOO!

MIAOOOOWW!

QUACK QUACK!

HONK!

bellowed the animals.

"Stop! Stop!" shouted Belle. "This is a lullaby. Do you want to scare everyone? Now let's try it again, softly this time. Ah-one, Ah-two..."

"Watch out!" barked Buster.
"Fox is about!"
Everyone was terrified.

"Ducklings! Stay close," quacked Mother Duck.

"What'll we do? What'll we do?" peeped the chicks, scurrying under their mother's wings.

"I'll kick him," said Daffodil.
"I'll bite him," said Trot.
"I'll hide up the oak tree and
drop down on him," said Squeaky.
"I'll butt him with my horns,"
said Billy the Kid.
Then Belle spoke.

"We want to frighten Fox
away for good," she said.
"And I've got an idea how."
The animals huddled together
and listened to Belle's plan.
"Agreed?" said Belle.
Everyone nodded.

Trot saw Fox first, sneaking through the big woods. He whinnied a warning.

"NEIGH!"

Gabby saw Fox slither into the orchard. She shouted a warning.

"HONK! HONK!"

Buster saw Fox creep into the farmyard, and head straight for the hen house. He barked a warning.

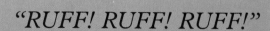

"RUFF! RUFF! RUFF!"

Belle banged on a bucket.
"NOW!" she squealed.
"BARNYARD HULLABALOO!"

MAAAAAAA

BAAAAAAA

MOOOOOOO

MIAOW

RUFF

QUACK QUACK

HONK

NEIGH

OINK

CLUCK CLUCK CLUCK

roared the animals.

They screeched, they snarled, they yowled and they caterwauled. They stomped their hooves and clattered their heels, shaking the ground.

Fox was so frightened that for a moment he could not move. Then he turned and ran, yelping in terror.

"Help! Monsters! Help! Help! Monsters at Potter's Barn! Help! Save me!"

"Hurray!" cheered the animals.

And from that day on, Barnyard Hullabaloo has been the Potter's Barn Band's favourite song.

As for Fox, he is still running.

Mish Mash
Hash

Making a cake for Belle was Gabby's idea.

"Belle works so hard conducting the Potter's Barn Band,"
said Gabby. "It would be a lovely surprise for her."

"She's gone to the Big Woods with Buster this morning,"
said Rosie the calf. "If we hurry, we can have the cake ready
before she gets back."

"Who knows how to make a cake?" said Henny-Penny.

No one spoke.

"It seems to me," said Daffodil, "that grass tastes extremely nice."

"You can't go wrong with oats," said Trot.

"Flies and seeds can't be beat," said the ducks.

"Worms and beetles are my best treat," said Red Rooster.

"My food is the tastiest," said Tam.

"No, ours," said the hens.

"No, mine," said Squeaky.

"I know," said Tilly. "Let's mix our favourite foods together. That way our cake will taste extra yummy!"
Everyone thought this was a great idea and ran off to collect the ingredients.

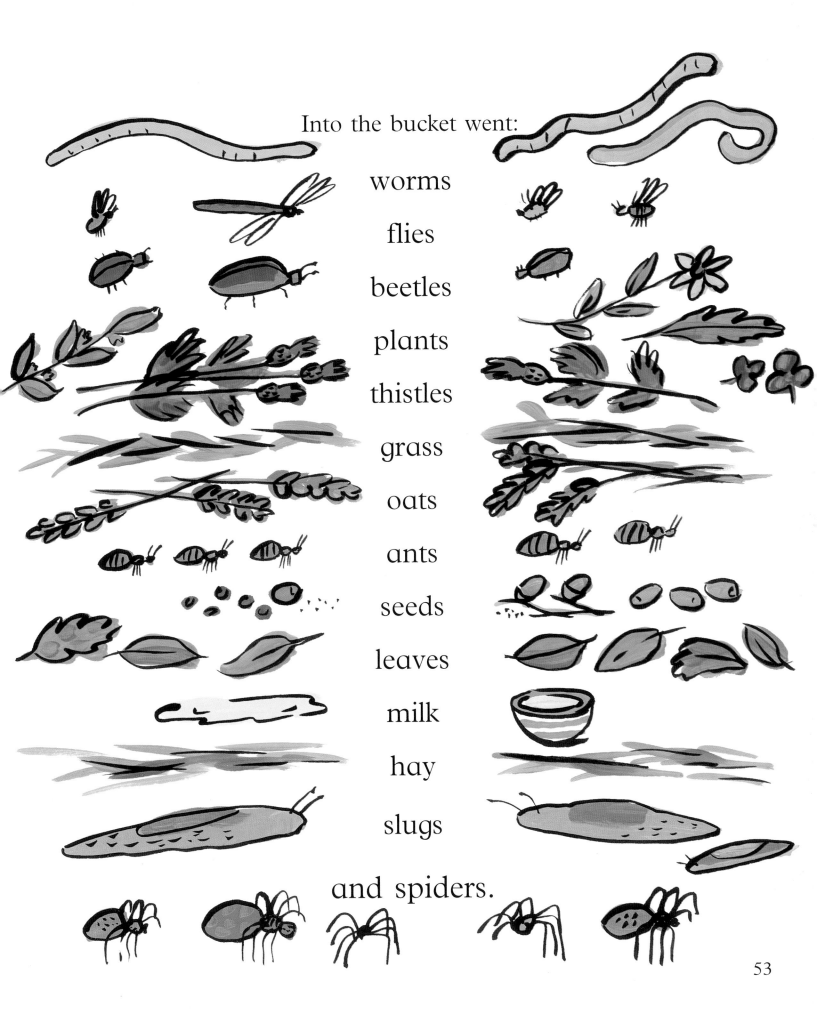

Into the bucket went:

worms

flies

beetles

plants

thistles

grass

oats

ants

seeds

leaves

milk

hay

slugs

and spiders.

"How about some nice cardboard?" said Billy the Kid.

"YUCK!" squealed Gabby.

"It was just an idea," said Billy.

"Now, mix!" shouted Tam.

SWISH SWASH SLOSH
SWISH SWASH SLOSH

Round and round and round they stirred, until at last the cake was mixed.

"Hmmm, doesn't that look delicious?" said the ducklings.

"I can't wait to taste it," said Rosie.

"Now," said Gabby. "We'll turn the cake out onto the ground and then decorate it."

Slowly and carefully, the animals tipped the bucket over.

SLIP SLOP SLIP SLOP

. . . . PLOP!

The cake slopped out of the bucket into a heap on the ground.
"Oh no!" wailed the lambs.

"Our lovely cake!" peeped the chicks.

"Why didn't it keep its shape?" moaned Gabby.

"Never mind," said Trot. "We've made something better than a cake. We've made Mish Mash Hash."

"Quick, Belle's coming," said Squeaky.
They decorated the Mish Mash Hash as fast as they could.

Belle wandered into the farmyard.
"What's going on?" she said.
"SURPRISE!" shouted the animals.
"It's for you, Belle," said Gabby.
"Thank you for all your hard work."

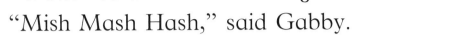
Belle smiled and smiled and smiled. Then she took a mouthful.
"Wow!" said Belle. "Tastes great! What is it?"
"Mish Mash Hash," said Gabby.
"Can I have the recipe?" said Belle.

"Sure," said Trot. "You add –

worms

flies

beetles

plants

thistles

grass

oats

ants

seeds

leaves

milk

hay

slugs

and spiders.

Stir! Slop! EAT!"

60

Chicks
Just Want
To Have Fun

Henny-Penny was tucking her chicks in for the night.

"It's not fair," cheeped the chicks. "It's not even dark yet. Why do we have to go to bed so early?"

"Because you're young and you need your rest," said Henny-Penny.

"But we're not sleepy," said the chicks.

"You will be soon," said Henny-Penny. "Now, no more chit-chat. Goodnight, chicks. Sleep tight."

And she closed the hen house door.

For a moment there was silence.

"It's not fair!"
said the black
speckled chick.

"I bet everyone else
is up having fun,"
said the red chick.

"I bet Belle is
dancing," said
the brown chick.

"I bet Billy the Kid
is playing football,"
said the yellow one.

"I bet Daffodil is
having a party,"
said the fluffy white.

The chicks looked at each other.
"Let's go and find out," they cheeped.
And they sneaked out of the hen house over to Belle's pen.
Belle was standing by the trough, singing her favourite song to her piglets.

A big fat pig

A big big fat pig

A big big big fat pig

A big big big big fat pig

A big big big fat pig

A big big fat pig

A big fat pig

A fat pig

A pig

Pig

Oink

"Not much fun here," whispered the brown chick. "Let's see what Billy the Kid is up to."

Off they pitter-pattered. Billy was in his shed talking to himself.

"Thank you, yes, I will have a fourth helping of those delicious cardboard boxes," he said.

"Not much fun here," peeped the yellow chick.

"There must be a party at the barn," said the black speckled chick.

Off they fluttered. A beam of light shone under a small crack at the bottom of the barn door.

"I hear voices," whispered the yellow chick.

The chicks squeezed underneath the door.

"Hi everybody! We're here! Let's party!" they cheeped.

Buster looked up from his cushion. Daffodil and Squeaky stopped talking. The ducks untucked their heads from under their wings. Mother Sheep opened her eyes.

"What are you doing here at this hour, chicks?" asked Daffodil.

"We're looking for the party," they peeped.

"What party?" said Daffodil.

"The party you have when we're asleep," said the fluffy white chick.

"We're much too tired to have a party," said Daffodil.

"So what are you doing?" said the yellow chick.

"Just chatting," said Squeaky.

"BORING!" cheeped the chicks.

"Hurry home now, before Henny-Penny finds you missing," said Daffodil.

The chicks filed sadly out of the barn.

"Good night everyone," they said, and crept back into the hen house.

"There must be a party, somewhere," said the brown chick.

"There is!" said the black speckled chick. "Right here!"

"What's going on in there?" called Henny-Penny.

"Nothing, Mum," said the chicks. "We're just getting sleepy."

Moo
Baa Baa
Quack

Potter's Barn gleamed. Daffodil and Rosie had swept the farmyard and Trot and Tam had tidied the barn. The ducks had even polished the old pump.

Today was a big day for the Potter's Barn Band. Friends from far and wide were coming to hear them sing their new song.

The band gathered in the barn for their final rehearsal. Everyone was very excited.

Belle stamped her trotter for attention. She looked lovely wearing a new blue bow.

"Everyone ready to sing 'Moo Baa Baa Quack'?"

"Yes!" shouted the animals.

"Does everyone remember the words?" asked Belle.

"I'm not sure," said Rosie.

So Belle sang the song.

Moo Baa Baa
Moo Baa Baa
Neigh Ne Neigh Ne Neigh
QUACK QUACK!

Moo Baa Baa
Moo Baa Baa
Neigh Ne Neigh Ne Neigh
QUACK QUACK!

"Remember ducklings, a nice loud *QUACK QUACK* at the end," said Belle.

"Easy peasy," said the ducklings.

"Good," said Belle. "Then let's take it from the top. One, two, three:

Moo Baa Baa
Moo - *QUACK! QUACK!*

"No, no ducklings," said Belle. "It's not your turn yet. You sing after Trot."

"Sorry, Belle," quacked the ducklings.

"Let's try it again," said Belle. "One, two, three:"

Moo Baa Baa
Moo Baa Baa
QUACK! QUACK!

"Ducklings," said Belle. "This is very simple. Wait for Trot. Then sing."

"Sorry, Belle," quacked the ducklings.

"One, two, three:"

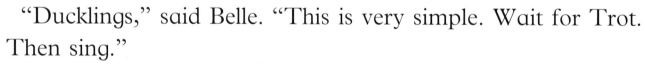

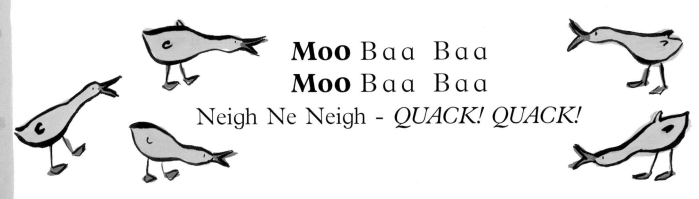

Moo Baa Baa
Moo Baa Baa
Neigh Ne Neigh - *QUACK! QUACK!*

"NO!" grunted Belle. "You sang too soon."

"We'll get it right next time, Belle," said the ducklings.

Belle tried not to get cross. Through the barn window she could see the audience gathering in the farmyard.

"Think, everybody!" squealed Belle. "How can we help the ducklings get it right?"

"I could nudge them when it's their turn to sing," said Rosie.

"No!" quacked the ducklings.

"I could poke them," said Trot.

"NO!" quacked the ducklings.

"I've got an idea, Belle," said Squeaky, who had been listening from the corner. "Why don't you look at them when it's their turn to sing?"

"Look at *them*?" said Belle. "But then the audience won't see my beautiful new bow."

Buster popped his head inside the barn.

"The audience is waiting," said Buster. "Good luck everyone."

"Okay," said Belle. "We'll do what Squeaky suggests." And she tried not to think about her beautiful blue bow.

"Give me your ribbon, Belle," said Squeaky. "I've got an idea."

Belle raised her snout and looked at the Potter's Barn Band.
Please ducklings, she thought, get it right.

"One, two, three," she counted. The animals opened their mouths and began to sing.

Baa **Moo Moo**
Neigh **Mooo** Baa
Baa Ba Ba Neigh **Moo**
QUACK! QUACK!

"Hurray! We got it right that time," quacked the ducklings, bouncing about in delight.

"But now the rest of you are muddled," hissed Belle. Then she sneaked a look at the audience. Everyone was smiling. No one had noticed all the mistakes.

Belle lifted her snout and started conducting again.

And this time . . .

> **Moo** B a a B a a
> **Moo** B a a B a a
> Neigh Ne Neigh Ne Neigh
> *QUACK QUACK!*

> **Moo** B a a B a a
> **Moo** B a a B a a
> Neigh Ne Neigh Ne Neigh
> *QUACK QUACK!*

"Bravo!" clapped the audience.
"Well done, everyone," said Belle. "Stand up and take your bow."